King & Kayla

and the Case of Found Fred

Written by
Dori Hillestad Butler

Illustrated by
Nancy Meyers

PEACHTREE
ATLANTA

For Ben and Artemis.
Sorry, the Case of Found Molly just doesn't have the
same ring as the Case of Found Fred.
—D. H. B.
For George.
May you grow up to love a boat ride as much
as your Great-Grandpa George.
—N. M.

Published by
PEACHTREE PUBLISHING COMPANY INC.
1700 Chattahoochee Avenue
Atlanta, Georgia 30318-2112
PeachtreeBooks.com

Text © 2019 by Dori Hillestad Butler
Illustrations © 2019 by Nancy Meyers

Edited by Kathy Landwehr
Design and composition by Nicola Simmonds Carmack
The illustrations were drawn in pencil, with color added digitally.

Printed in January 2022 by Toppan Leefung Printing Limited in China
10 9 8 7 6 5 4 3 2 (hardcover)
10 9 8 7 6 (trade paperback)

HC ISBN: 978-1-68263-052-5
PB ISBN: 978-1-68263-053-2

Library of Congress Cataloging-in-Publication Data

Names: Butler, Dori Hillestad, author. | Meyers, Nancy, 1961– illustrator.
Title: King & Kayla and the case of found Fred / written by Dori Hillestad Butler ;
illustrated by Nancy Meyers.
Other titles: King and Kayla and the case of the found Fred
Description: Atlanta : Peachtree Publishers, [2019] | Summary: Kayla's dog King
becomes the lead detective in the case of the lost dog in search of his human family.
Identifiers: LCCN 2018003501| ISBN 9781682630525 (hardcover) | ISBN 9781682630532
(trade pbk.)
Subjects: | CYAC: Dogs—Fiction. | Lost and found possessions—Fiction. |
Human-animal communication—Fiction. | Mystery and detective stories.
Classification: LCC PZ7.B9759 Kg 2019 | DDC [E]—dc23 LC record available at
https://lccn.loc.gov/2018003501

Contents

Chapter One

Grandma's House

Hello!

My name is King. I'm a dog. This is Kayla. She is my human.

Kayla and I are on vacation at Grandma's house. I LOVE Grandma's house. It's my favorite place!

"Look, King!" Kayla calls. "I've got the ball!"

Kayla throws the ball into the lake.

SPLASH!

"Got it! I've got the ball!"

I swim…swim…SWIM to shore.

I shake myself off and bring
Kayla the ball.

Sniff…sniff…

I smell someone! Someone
I've never smelled before.

Look! It's a new friend!

"Hello!" I say. "I'm King. What's your name?"

"Fred," he says.

Fred smells like smoke and
hamburgers. I LOVE hamburgers.
They're my favorite food!

Kayla comes over. "Well, hello," she says to Fred. "What's your name?"

Fred backs away.

"Don't be scared," I tell Fred. "This is Kayla. She is my human."

Kayla feels Fred's neck. "You don't
have a collar," she says.

"It came off when I ran under a fence,"
Fred says.

Kayla doesn't understand.

"Do you have people?" I ask.

"Yes, but I lost them during the big, BIG booms!" Fred says.

"That was five or one nights ago," I say. "That was a SCARY night!"

"I know," Fred says.

"Don't worry," I say. "Kayla and I are detectives! We can help you find your people."

Chapter Two

Fred Is Not a Stray

"You smell smoky," Kayla tells Fred.

"That's because my people had a
bonfire," Fred says.

Kayla doesn't understand a word Fred
says. "Do you know whose dog this is?"
she asks Grandma.

"No," Grandma says. "Maybe he's a
stray."

"I'm not a stray," Fred says. He paws at Kayla's lap.

"Do you want to shake hands?" she asks.

"Okay," Fred says. He lifts a paw.

Kayla shakes it.

"What else can you
do?" Kayla asks.
"Can you sit?"

Fred and I both sit.

"Down!" Kayla says.

Fred and I both lie down.

"This dog isn't a stray," Kayla tells Grandma. "He can shake hands, sit, and lie down."

"You're a good detective, honey," Grandma says.

"Thank you," Kayla says. "King is a detective, too. We'll solve this case. We'll find this dog's family."

"How?" Grandma asks.

"We can start by talking to your neighbors," Kayla says.

We visit all the houses on Grandma's dirt road.

"Have you seen this dog before?" Kayla asks the people at each house.

"Do you know who he belongs to?"

No one does.

We go back to Grandma's house.

"Let's make some posters," Kayla says.

Fred and I help.

Kayla and Grandma staple the posters
to mailboxes, fence posts, and trees.

"I hope your family sees these posters
and calls us," Kayla says to Fred.

"Me too," Fred says.

Chapter Three

Fred's Clue

Nine or three days go by.

No one calls about Fred.

"We need a clue," Kayla says. "A clue would help us find this dog's family."

"Do you have any clues?" I ask Fred.

"No," he says.

But sometimes you can have a clue
and not even know it.

"Is your house by the lake or by the
road?" I ask Fred.

"Neither," says Fred. "It's in a big
building."

"There aren't any big buildings around here," I say.

"I know," says Fred. "We live far, far away. We're here on vacation. We're staying at a campground."

"You're staying at a campground?" I say. "That's a clue!"

Kayla grabs a notebook and pencil.

"Let's make a list of everything we *know* about this case," she says.

1. This dog doesn't have a collar or any tags.

2. He can sit, lie down, and shake hands.

3. No one on Grandma's dirt road knows who he is.

If I could write, I would add this to
Kayla's list of things we *know*:

Fred's family is staying
at a campground.

"Now, let's make a list of what we *don't know* about the case," Kayla says.

1. Where did this dog come from?

2. Where is his family?

3. How did he get here?

If I could write, I would add this to
Kayla's list of things we *don't know*:

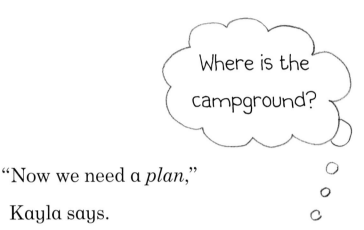

Where is the
campground?

"Now we need a *plan*,"
Kayla says.

I have a *plan*:

Find the
campground!

Chapter Four

Boat Ride!

"Do you know where the campground is?" I ask Grandma. "Can you take us to the campground?"

"King!" Kayla cries. "Paws on the floor!"

I whisper in Kayla's ear. "Campground!
Campground! Campground!"

"Do you need to go outside?" she asks.

"Yes," I say. Campgrounds are outside!

"Our campground is by the lake,"
Fred says. "Is that a clue?"

"Yes," I say.

But this is a BIG lake. How do we find
a campground on a big lake?

"Grandma," Kayla says. "Look at all the people on the lake. Maybe one of them knows this little dog."

"Let's take a boat ride and see what we can find out," Grandma says.

Oh, boy! I LOVE boat rides. They're my favorite thing!

We all get in the boat. *Zoom*! Grandma drives us around the lake.

"Hello? Excuse me?" Kayla shouts to a fisherman. "Do you know this dog? We're trying to find his family."

"No, sorry," the fisherman calls back.

All of a sudden, Fred yells, "THERE'S
OUR CAMPGROUND!" He climbs on
the edge of the boat and...

SPLASH!

Fred jumps in the lake.

"Wait for me!" I yell.

SPLASH!

I jump in the lake, too.

"King! Little Dog!
NO!" Kayla yells.

"Let's go find my
people!" Fred says.

Chapter Five

Where Is Fred's Family?

Fred and I swim and swim…until our paws touch the sand.

"Doggy!" A small boy points.

"Do you see your people?" I ask Fred.

"No," Fred says. "But I smell them!"

"What do they smell like?" I ask.

"They smell like my people!" Fred says.

Fred follows a scent. I follow Fred.

We go up the beach, across the grass, and over to a tent.

"Mom! Dad! Max! I'm back!" Fred paws at the tent.

A boy crawls out. "FRED!" he cries.

A man and lady come out, too. They hug and kiss Fred all over.

"Thanks for helping me find my people," Fred says.

"You're welcome," I say.

But now I'm afraid I've lost MY people! Where are Kayla and Grandma?

I hear a voice.

"King? Where are you, King?"

It's Kayla!

"Right here," I call back. I follow
Kayla's voice.

Kayla and Grandma are on the dock.
I run to them.

"There you are, King," Kayla says. "I can't believe you jumped in the lake!"

"Sorry," I say.

"It looks like that little dog found his family," Grandma says.

"And I found you and Kayla,"
I say.

I LOVE Kayla and Grandma. They're my favorite thing!

The End

Oh, boy! I LOVE books.
They're my favorite things!

"A delightful series start that will have kids returning to read more about Kayla and King. It's also a great introduction to mysteries, gathering facts, and analytical thinking for an unusually young set." —*Booklist*

"A perfect option for newly independent readers ready to start transitioning from easy readers to beginning chapter books." —*School Library Journal*

"Readers will connect with this charmingly misunderstood pup (along with his exasperated howls, excited tail wagging, and sheepish grins)." —*Kirkus Reviews*

King & Kayla and the Case of the Missing Dog Treats

HC: 978-1-56145-877-6
PB: 978-1-68263-015-0

King & Kayla and the Case of the Mysterious Mouse

HC: 978-1-56145-879-0
PB: 978-1-68263-017-4

King & Kayla and the Case of the Secret Code

HC: 978-1-56145-878-3
PB: 978-1-68263-016-7

King & Kayla and the Case of the Lost Tooth

HC: 978-1-56145-880-6
PB: 978-1-68263-018-1